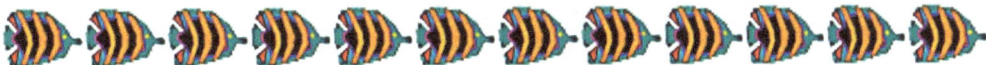

My Lil' Big Ocean

Publishing Information & Credits

Toby A. Williams, Published May 2019

All rights reserved. This book, or parts thereof, may not be reproduced in any form without written permission from the Publisher.

This is a fictional children's story and not based on any actual person, place, or event (living or deceased). Any resemblance is entirely coincidental.

ISBN: 978-0-9600499-3-6

Written by Author, Toby A. Williams
Illustrated by Award-winning Artist, Corrina Holyoake
Edited by Author & Poet, Sue Campion

The BROOKE LYNN Adventures Series

My Lil' Ladybug Friend, Released December 2018 (Book 1)
My Lil' Big Ocean, Released May 2019 (Book 2)
My Lil' First School, Releasing Fall 2019 (Book 3

My Lil' Big Ocean

A frightful splash it makes in its wake,
    enough to scare the little fish!
Whatever could its loud roar mean?
    Maybe it's friendly? Oh, I so wish!

While calm and quiet, it invites me in,
    drawing me closer to the shore.
Lest I dare stick my big toe in,
    or, back up two steps, maybe more?

My Lil' Big Ocean

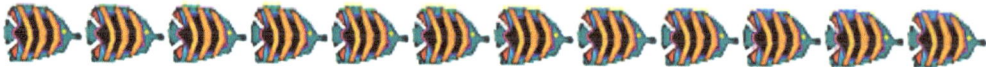

My Lil' Big Ocean

Hello *again friend, Brooke Lynn here,*
      explorer of all things unknown.
Such is my new **wavy** wonder,
      yet, we needn't go it alone!

Join me on this coastal adventure,
      where wet and wild come alive.
It's sure to please all our senses,
      after one long, scenic drive.

My Lil' Big Ocean

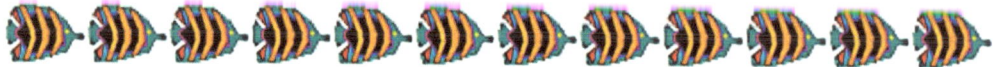

My Lil' Big Ocean

Late, on a hot evening in June,
       Mom turned her smiling face just so,
"What about a beach day, Brooke Lynn?
       Possibly soon, how's tomorrow?"

"Of course!", I excitedly stumbled,
       then jumped up so high – don't fall!
"Can I bring my new pail and shovel?
       My sandcastle will stand so tall."

I've heard the sea is so large and blue,
       with the smell of salt in the air.
Is it gentle and friendly in nature,
       or, fierce and strong like a bear?!

My Lil' Big Ocean

My Lil' Big Ocean

My tote bag was ready, almost full,
      and yet, I hadn't even begun.
"Oh Mom, what else should I bring?"
      Whew, much to do before I'm done!

The morning came rather quickly,
      and soon we'd be at the coast.
"Brooke, please finish your oatmeal,
      drink your juice and eat your toast!"

Excitement filled up my heart,
      while deciding what else to bring.
My swimsuit, a bucket, a towel or two,
      maybe if I could, just one more thing?

My Lil' Big Ocean

My Lil' Big Ocean

My thoughts were running wild,
      with such a list, oh what a chore!
I imagined the big waves crashing,
      down hard against the seashore.

Mom filled the picnic basket,
      full of goodies, all neat and trim.
I chimed, "Mom, need any help?"
      "Nope", as she stuffed it to the brim.

My Lil' Big Ocean

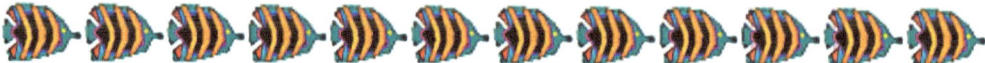

My Lil' Big Ocean

Mom said quickly with a big breath,
    "Now hurry, let's go get ready.
Such a long ride to the shore,
    the traffic should be slow but steady."

The car was packed, all loaded up,
    with beach bags, oh too much gear!
I jumped through the open car door,
    and sat buckled calmly in the rear.

My Lil' Big Ocean

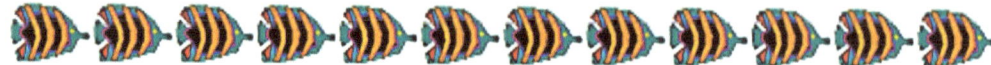

My Lil' Big Ocean

We drove for hours and many miles,
      "How much longer 'til we arrive?
Mom, oh please, are we there yet?
      It's such a winding long drive!"

Then suddenly, without a clue,
      we rounded a turn and a bend.
It was larger than I ever thought;
      was this ocean without an end?

Fresh smell of sea air sailed up my nose,
      with the roar of each crashing wave.
It gave way to a new excitement,
      let's not pretend, must be brave!

My Lil' Big Ocean

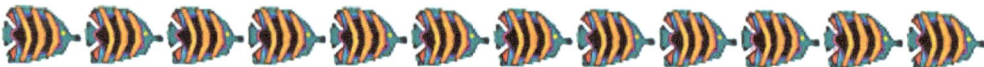

My Lil' Big Ocean

Quickly unloading our beach gear,
    we found a spot nearest the shore.
With umbrella now pitched in the sand,
    I suddenly saw seashells galore!

Seagulls came swooping and soaring,
    then climbing way up to such height.
I watched bodies swimming and bobbing,
    "Pinch me," as I twirled with delight.

I grabbed my bucket and headed out,
    down toward the water's edge.
When my eyes spotted a lil' tide-pool,
    by the rocks off the jetty ledge.

My Lil' Big Ocean

My Lil' Big Ocean

What a treasure! So many fishy fish!
    Will they all fit in my new pail?
An oyster, a clam, a clear jellyfish,
    even a seahorse with a tail!

Oh, here's something strange and new,
    which leaves a slimy, slick trail.
Look, it creeps along the smooth rocks,
    crouch closer, why it's a sea snail!

One more creature shall I find,
    before my pail is full of treasure?
Maybe just the sight of one whale,
    or a dolphin for my pleasure?

My Lil' Big Ocean

My Lil' Big Ocean

I wandered back and forth to our spot,
    grabbing a quick snack and cold drink.
As Mom sunned in her beach chair,
    a seagull snatched my chips in a blink!

Mom sat up, "Brooke Lynn, shall we swim?
    Let's go in for a nice, cool dip."
Smiling, I hurried right beside her,
    and held her hand with a tight grip.

And slowly we walked into the water,
    just up to our knees – then froze.
All the way in, yikes, my body tingled,
    down to my feet and popsicle toes!

My Lil' Big Ocean

My Lil' Big Ocean

Swimming, then springing off the sand,
    I glided atop the ocean.
When the tide pushed me toward the shore,
    I swam in a dog-paddle motion.

Splashing, I dashed to catch a wave,
    then over and under with the flow.
The waves became strong, pushing me down,
    while I swam from the under-tow.

Mom said, "Time to take a break,
    before our hands turn into prunes.
Brooke Lynn, have you found enough shells?
    Maybe over by the sand dunes?"

My Lil' Big Ocean

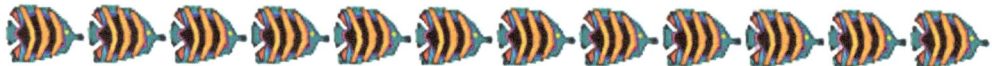

My Lil' Big Ocean

I plopped down onto my towel,
    where my beach ball sat deflated,
Mom took deep breaths 'til it was full,
    bouncing high – we were elated!

Time to fill my buckets with sand,
    to build the biggest sandcastle.
Mom soon joined in the digging,
    'twas such fun and nary a hassle.

Finished, we stared at our kingdom,
    with a moat and quite a tall tower.
When the tide crept up too close,
    the castle was gone in an hour!

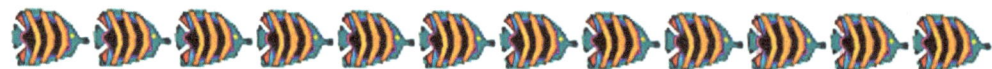

My Lil' Big Ocean

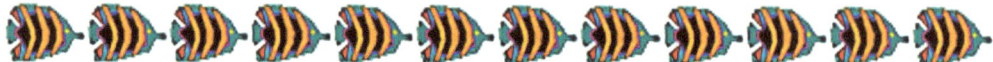

My Lil' Big Ocean

Mom perked up, "Before we leave,
    there's something I want you to see.
It's a short swift walk from here, Brooke,
    near the pier, just for you and me."

Mom steered us to the long boardwalk,
    then stopped at the Penny Arcade.
We played a dart game and ring toss,
    while slurping a sweet lemonade.

Salt-water taffy, cotton candy,
    too many delicious delights.
The rush of the noise and crowds,
    drew attention to yonder lights.

My Lil' Big Ocean

My Lil' Big Ocean

As we turned the corner to see,
    I hugged extra close to Mom's side.
There stood the biggest Ferris Wheel,
    inviting us to take a ride.

We got in line and inched real close,
    as I grabbed Mom's hand real tight.
It took us up so high – what a view!
    Mom yelled, "Everything's in our sight!"

Weary, we walked back along the shore,
    trying to capture this moment.
I closed my eyes to hold the memory,
    all for my lasting enjoyment.

My Lil' Big Ocean

My Lil' Big Ocean

One last sea shell, oh there it is,
      staring back at me...just for Mom!
I heard Mom loudly say, "Thank you!"
      as the crashing sea turned to calm.

Mom stopped, stared o'er the water and asked,
      "Brooke Lynn, how's your first ocean trip?
Is it what you dreamed it would be?"
      "Yes, and more!", as I took a sip.

My Lil' Big Ocean

My Lil' Big Ocean

I picked up one last beach toy,
    my shells safely in a glass jar.
When both legs grew tired and heavy,
    I slowly slumbered to the car.

"Mom, my first time at the ocean,
    it's much more than I EVER thought.
I love you for taking me – **thanks**.
    This beach day truly meant a lot!"

The End

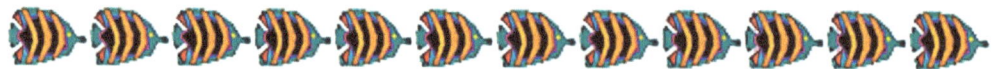

My Lil' Big Ocean

My Lil' Big Ocean

Factoids About Oceans

The ocean is home to some incredible creatures. How many different fish can you name? And, how many total fish are in the ocean? Wow, there are just too many to count since we've only explored about 5% of the world's oceans. There's a lot more to be discovered!

Around 70% of the Earth's surface is covered by oceans. There is a total of five oceans with the largest ocean, the Pacific Ocean, winning the prize. Try to name the other four (see Answers below).

Hold your breath as you dunk under the waves. When you pop back up, the air you take into your lungs may be from that ocean. About 70% of the oxygen we breathe each day is produced by the oceans.

Along the ocean floor, there are mountains, large canyons, deep trenches, and even a large reef that can be seen from the Moon! It's called the Great Barrier Reef and is home to some incredible fish. It's Earth's largest living structure. The reef is alive just like you!

- *(Answers: Atlantic Ocean, Indian Ocean, Arctic Ocean and Southern Ocean)*
- *Note: National Geographic referenced for these ocean tidbits.*

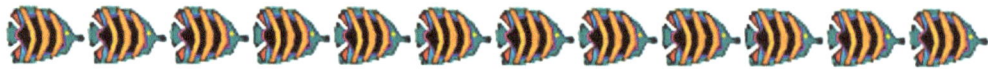

My Lil' Big Ocean

Book Review

If you enjoyed this book, please consider leaving an honest Review on Amazon.com or drop me a line at the e-mail address of tawilms@outlook.com. Your interest in children's literature and literacy is much appreciated.

You may also be interested in **My Lil' Ladybug Friend**, The BROOKE LYNN Adventures series, Book 1. Available for sale now on Amazon.com.

For more information about this series, visit my Author Page: amazon.com/author/tobywilliams, or follow me on Facebook @**The Brooke Lynn Adventures** to see what is coming soon.

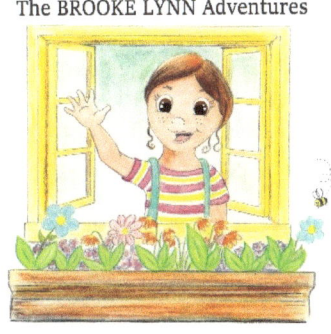

Thank you for coming along on this ocean adventure.

- **Toby A. Williams**

CPSIA information can be obtained
at www.ICGtesting.com
Printed in the USA
LVHW070527150819
627744LV00013B/225/P